Accelerated Reader™
ATOS™ 3.0 – 3.9

TRAPPED ON THE D.C. TRAIN!

by Ron Roy
illustrated by Timothy Bush

A STEPPING STONE BOOK™
Random House New York

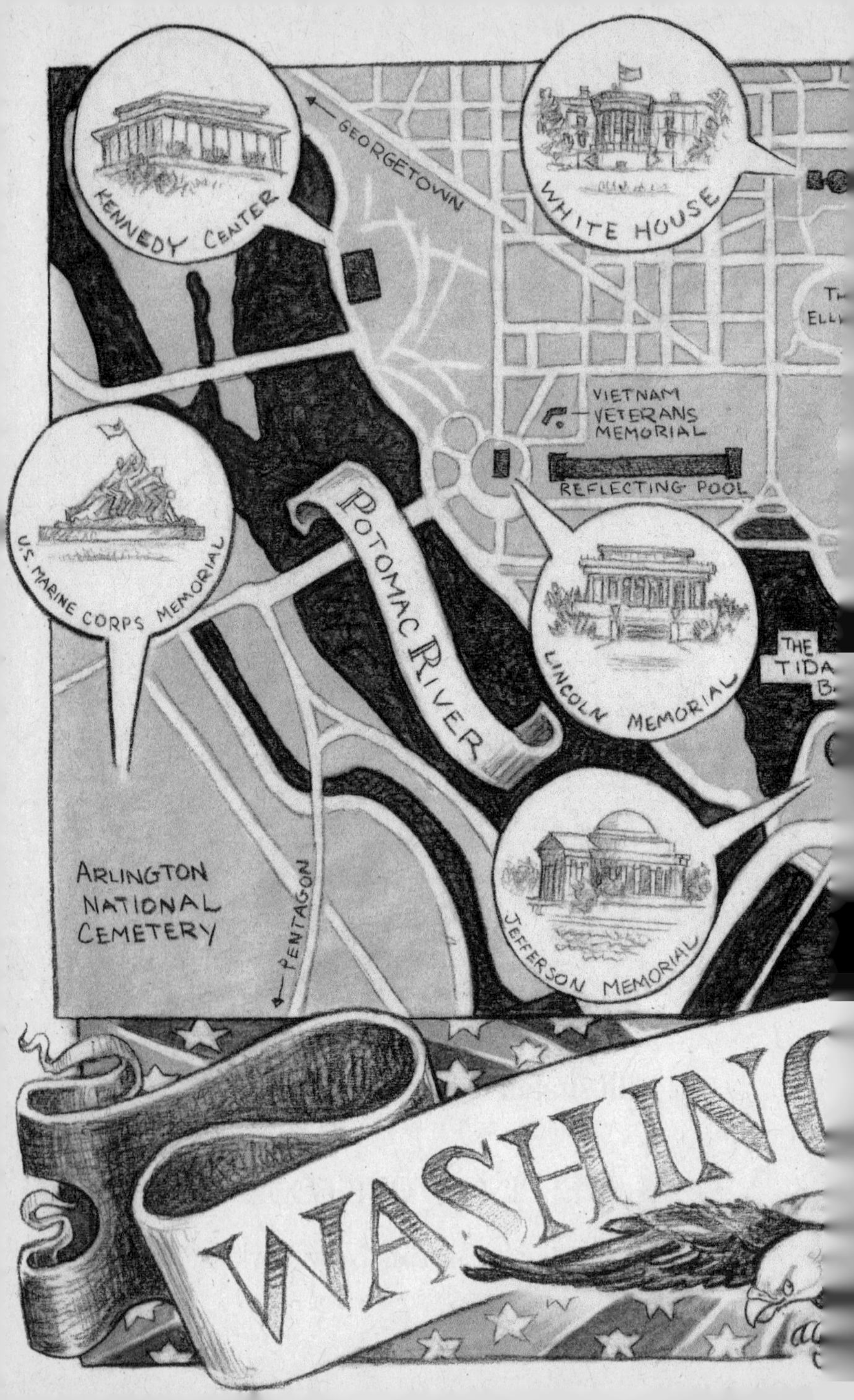
KENNEDY CENTER
GEORGETOWN
WHITE HOUSE
VIETNAM
VETERANS
MEMORIAL
REFLECTING POOL
U.S. MARINE CORPS MEMORIAL
POTOMAC RIVER
LINCOLN MEMORIAL
JEFFERSON MEMORIAL
ARLINGTON
NATIONAL
CEMETERY
PENTAGON

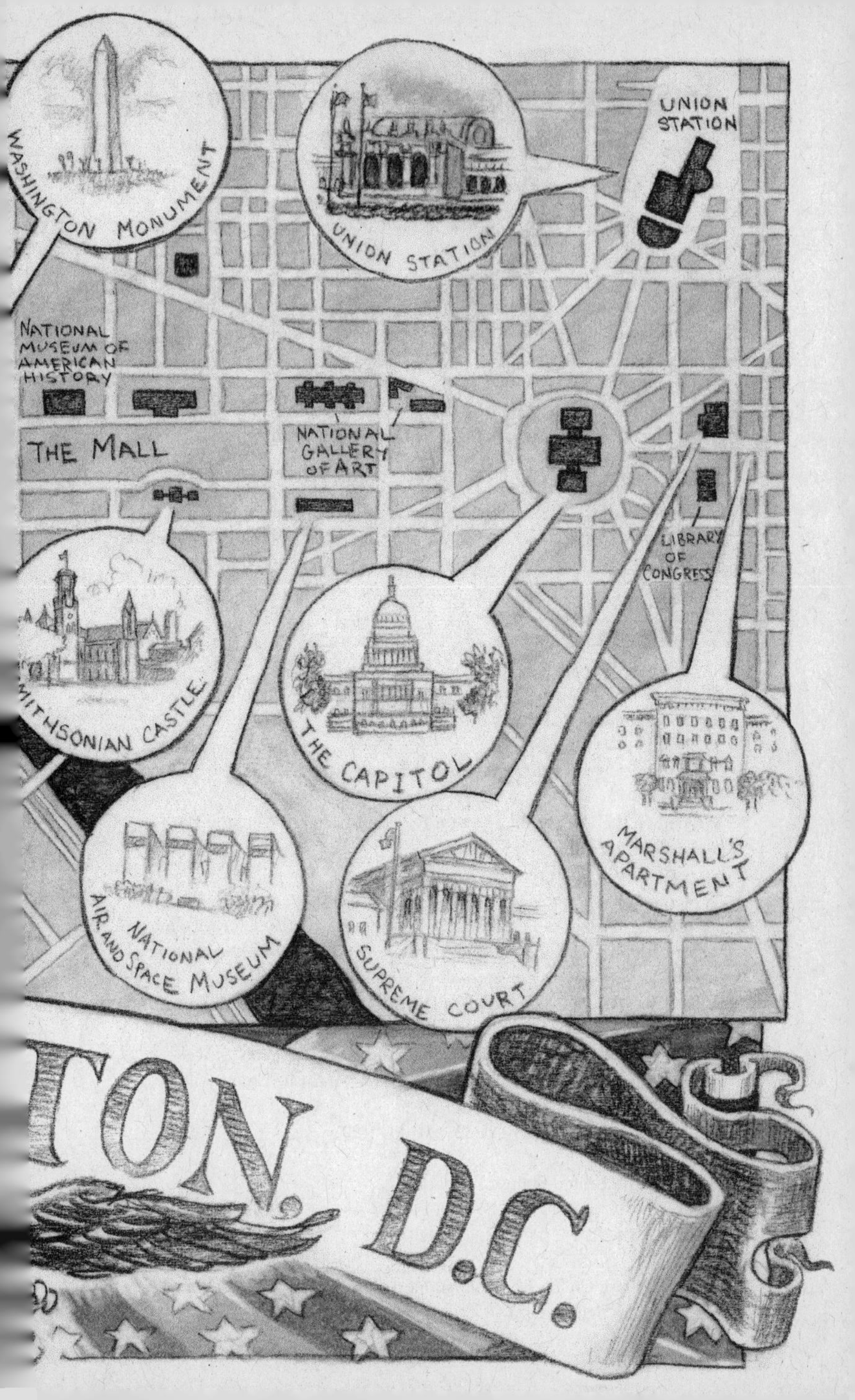
WASHINGTON MONUMENT
UNION STATION
UNION STATION
NATIONAL MUSEUM OF AMERICAN HISTORY
THE MALL
NATIONAL GALLERY OF ART
LIBRARY OF CONGRESS
SMITHSONIAN CASTLE
THE CAPITOL
MARSHALL'S APARTMENT
NATIONAL AIR AND SPACE MUSEUM
SUPREME COURT
TON. D.C.

This book is for my readers, every one.
—R.R.

Photo credits: pp. 88–89, courtesy of the Library of Congress.

SteppingStonesBooks.com
www.randomhouse.com/kids

Educators and librarians, for a variety of teaching tools, visit us at
www.randomhouse.com/teachers

Library of Congress Cataloging-in-Publication Data
Roy, Ron.
Trapped on the D.C. train! / by Ron Roy ; illustrated by Timothy Bush ;
[cover illustration by Greg Swearingen].
p. cm. — (Capital mysteries ; 13)
"A Stepping Stone book."
Summary: On a trip to Pennsylvania, presidential stepdaughter KC Corcoran and her friend Marshall are exploring the rest of the train when the special caboose at the back disappears—along with the Vice President.
ISBN 978-0-375-85926-7 (pbk.) — ISBN 978-0-375-95926-4 (lib. bdg.) —
ISBN 978-0-375-89815-0 (ebook)
[1. Mystery and detective stories. 2. Railroad trains—Fiction. 3. Vice-Presidents—Fiction. 4. Kidnapping—Fiction.] I. Bush, Timothy, ill.
II. Swearingen, Greg, ill. III. Title.
PZ7.R8139Tp 2011 [Fic]—dc22 2010030129

Printed in the United States of America

10 9 8 7 6 5 4 3 2 1

Contents

UNION STAT

1
Union Station Rocks

"This place is huge!" Marshall said. "The ceiling must be a hundred feet high!"

KC Corcoran and her best friend, Marshall Li, were hurrying through Union Station, Washington's large train station. They followed Mary Kincaid, the vice president of the United States, through the crowd of people.

With them were two secret service agents. A muscular man named Robert walked next to the vice president. The other agent, Janet, was right behind KC and Marshall.

"I read that it once was the biggest train station in the world," KC said.

Both KC and Marshall gawked at the sights as they followed the vice president. Shops and restaurants lined the sides of the cavernous station. It was nearly seven in the evening, and thousands of people were going home after work. Some, like KC and Marshall, were heading for trains. Others were shopping, eating, or just sightseeing. In one area, a small band had people dancing.

"I hope the train is air-conditioned, too," Marshall said. It was June 15 and already hot in Washington. Marshall and KC both wore shorts and T-shirts and carried backpacks. KC's hair was tucked up under a baseball cap.

"It will be," KC said. "We're riding in a special car."

"It's cool of the vice president to invite

us to her farm for the weekend," said Marshall. "Does she have animals?"

Marshall loved animals of all kinds. But his favorites were spiders and insects. At home, he kept a pet tarantula named Spike.

"I know she has a dog named Bounder, and I think she has a couple of horses," KC said. "Maybe she'll let us ride them!"

"I've never ridden a horse," Marshall said.

The vice president turned around and smiled at the kids. "Almost there," she said. "I told you this place was gigantic! You're doing a good job keeping up."

Vice President Mary Kincaid wore dark glasses and a summer dress. A scarf covered her hair. She looked like any tourist.

"Is the vice president in disguise?" Marshall whispered to KC.

KC nodded. "She doesn't want people to recognize her when she goes to her farm on the weekends."

"Why not?"

"The president thinks she could get kidnapped, like he did last year," KC said.

"Is that why your hair is hidden today?" Marshall said. "So no one will know you're the president's stepdaughter?"

KC grinned. "Do I look like a boy?"

"Sort of," Marshall said. "A boy with a lot of freckles."

The vice president stopped at the top of an escalator. "Our train is on the track at the bottom," Mary Kincaid said. They all stepped onto the moving stairs. It took only a minute to reach the train platform. It was crowded with people and luggage.

"Boy, it's hot down here," Marshall said.

"What happened to the air-conditioning?"

"That's only upstairs," Mary Kincaid said. "But don't worry, our car will be very comfortable!" She pointed at the train waiting a few yards away. "There it is. Ours is the last car, the one with the little platform on the end."

"It's so cute!" KC said. "It looks like the caboose in a book I just read."

"I think it *was* a caboose once upon a time," Janet said. Like the others in the group, she was dressed casually. No one would guess she was a U.S. secret service agent. "A few years ago, the train company converted it into a special car. A lot of senators and congresspeople ride in it when they take this train. The vice president uses it at least once a month when she goes home."

The car was painted a dark, rich green. There were windows on the side with the blinds pulled down. Steps led up to a private door. The car was hitched to the end of a string of train cars, where other passengers were boarding.

"I didn't know you could take dogs on a train," Marshall said. He was watching a German shepherd standing next to a man wearing sunglasses.

"It's a Seeing Eye dog," KC said.

The dog wore a special harness and leash. The man carried a satchel with a large book poking out the top.

"And I'll bet that's a Braille book he's carrying," KC added.

A tall conductor helped the blind man and his dog up the steps of the train car just ahead of the vice president's special

TRACK 4

car. Once the man and dog were safely aboard, the conductor pulled a red bandana from his back pocket and wiped sweat from his bald head.

He smiled at KC. "Hot," he said. "But the whole train is cool inside."

Robert assisted the vice president up into their car. KC went next, followed by Marshall. Janet came aboard last.

KC took a deep breath of the cool air. She yanked her baseball cap off. Her red hair tumbled down to her shoulders.

"Wow!" Marshall said, taking in the car. "This is fancy!" The wide seats were soft and covered in dark blue leather. Each one had its own window and a small folding table. Above the seats were racks for luggage.

KC dropped her backpack on one of

the seats. "You want the window or aisle?" she asked Marshall.

"Window," Marshall said. "Then we can switch later." He reached over to raise the shade.

"I think we should keep them down until we leave the station," KC whispered. "The vice president doesn't want anyone to see who's in this car."

Mary Kincaid chose the seats farthest from the front of the car. She sat facing the door and kept her dark glasses and scarf in place. The two agents sat side by side in front of her.

KC turned around. "Ms. Kin . . . I mean Auntie Kitty, how far is it to your farm in Pennsylvania?"

KC and Marshall had been instructed not to call Mary Kincaid by her real name while they were on the train. So for the trip, she was Aunt Kitty, and the two agents were Kitty's sister and her husband. KC had also been told not to mention to any strangers that her stepfather was the President of the United States.

"A little more than an hour and a half," Mary Kincaid said. "Plenty of time to relax or snooze!"

"Are we stopping anywhere?" KC asked.

"No, this is an express train," Mary Kincaid said. "It goes straight through."

Just then the door to the car opened. A whoosh of air blew in. A man wearing dark blue uniform pants and a short-sleeved white shirt stepped into the car. He had curly hair and a wide mustache. KC figured that he was a conductor.

"Everyone settled?" he asked.

"Yes, thank you," the vice president said. "We're very comfortable. How much longer before we leave?"

"Just a few minutes," the man said. "But we've . . ."

Suddenly the lights went out in the little car.

KC heard the vice president gasp.

She also heard the two agents leap to their feet. KC knew they were standing in front of Mary Kincaid to protect her.

Someone grabbed KC's arm.

2
Train Troubles

"What happened?" Janet asked.

It was totally dark. The station platform was well lit, but no light came through the heavy window shades in their car. KC felt goose bumps tickle her arms.

"I was just about to tell you," the conductor said. "We have a small electrical problem but . . ."

The lights came on.

". . . it's nothing to worry about, just a short circuit somewhere," he continued. "It's happened a couple of times today. We have a technician looking at it."

"Thank you," the vice president said.

"If the lights go out while we're moving,

stay seated," the conductor went on. "The engineer will probably slow or stop the train for a few minutes."

KC glanced at Marshall. "Hey, Marsh, can I have my arm back?" she asked.

Marshall grinned. "I was protecting you," he said, removing his hand.

KC rolled her eyes. She turned to look behind her. The vice president was calmly listening to the conductor. She had removed her dark glasses. Janet and Robert were standing in front of her.

The conductor nodded at everyone. "Have a good trip," he said, and closed the door.

A moment later, the train began to move out of Union Station.

"Well, that was exciting!" Mary Kincaid said. The two agents smiled, nodded, and sat down. The vice president began texting on a cell phone.

KC raised the shade so that she and Marshall could watch the city of Washington zip by them out the window. Soon they were passing farmhouses, green fields, and trees.

"This is my first time on a train," Marshall told KC. "It's awesome!"

"I was on one once before," KC said. "When my mom was still married to my real father. We took a train down to Florida."

"Let's go out on that little porch thing!" Marshall said.

"Let me ask," KC said. She walked back to Mary Kincaid's seat. "Excuse me, can Marshall and I go out on the platform?"

The vice president smiled. "Sure.

Robert, will you go with them, please?"

The tall agent stood up. He followed KC and Marshall to the end of their car. KC opened the door, and they stepped onto the little porch. The floor had green carpeting, and the railing was black metal. Hot summer wind blew their hair all around as they stood and watched the city disappear.

"I feel like we're flying!" Marshall yelled over the wind.

The kids pointed out old barns and funny buildings, but it was hard to talk over the noise of the wind and the train. Just before they reached a crossing, the conductor blew a piercing whistle. KC held her hands over her ears.

Robert tapped KC on the shoulder. "Let's go back inside, miss," he said.

"Okay, thanks, Robert," KC said. They stepped into the car and sat down. KC tucked her long hair back under her hat.

"Does anyone want anything from the snack car?" the vice president asked. "I could use some coffee. Maybe a sandwich."

"Do they have cookies?" Marshall asked.

"I'm sure they have everything," Mary Kincaid said. "Janet? Robert?"

"Yes, ma'am," they both said.

"May we go get it?" KC asked.

The vice president hesitated. "I guess that would be okay," she said. "The snack car is two cars after this one."

"Should I go with them?" Janet asked.

"Oh, I think they'll be fine, Janet," Mary Kincaid said. "We're on a moving train, and the car is only a hundred feet away."

KC pulled a small pad and pencil from her backpack. She wanted to be a TV journalist after college, and she always carried something to write with. She made a list of five names: KITTY, JANET, ROBERT, MARSHALL, ME. After ME, she wrote ORANGE JUICE.

"What do you want, Marshall?" KC asked.

"Grape soda and cookies," he said.

KC wrote down the order.

"What an efficient waitress!" the vice president said. "I'll have coffee with cream, no sugar, please. Oh, and a tuna sandwich if they have it."

"A coffee, please," Janet said. "Black."

"Same for me," Robert said.

"Here's some money," the vice president said. She handed Janet a twenty-dollar bill. Janet passed it to KC.

KC slipped the money into the pocket of her shorts. "See you in a few minutes!" she told the others. She pulled her cap on and tucked her hair under it. "Let's go, Marsh."

Marshall opened the door at the end of the car. KC felt the warm air blow over her face.

Between the two cars was a small platform. It connected their car to the next. They could feel the train's wheels vibrating beneath the platform floor. They heard the wind rushing by. Straight ahead was another door.

Marshall shoved it open, and they found themselves in the next passenger car. The first seat on the right was occupied by the blind man they'd seen earlier. He sat facing the back of the train with his book on his lap. The Seeing Eye dog lay on the floor with its chin resting on the man's feet.

Across the aisle from the blind man, a woman slept in her seat, facing KC and Marshall. She had a small blanket bunched up around her shoulders and neck. KC could barely see the woman's face, just her closed eyes.

KC and Marshall walked slowly through the car. There were about ten other passengers. Most were working on laptops or chatting on cell phones. A couple were doing both at the same time. The rest were sleeping, reading, or staring out the windows at the sunset.

"Doesn't it feel weird walking through a moving train?" Marshall asked. "It's like my feet are asleep!"

"It'll be even worse when we come back

carrying the stuff!" KC said. Her body swayed as she tried to keep her balance.

They passed a conductor. It was the same one they'd seen outside the train. He moved out of the way so the kids could pass.

"Going for snacks?" he asked.

"Yes," KC said. "Are we close?"

"Next car," the man said. He used his bandana to wipe his bald head, then stuffed it into his back pocket. When he turned around, the hankie looked like a red tail.

Before KC and Marshall moved another inch, the lights went out.

"Oh no, not again," the conductor muttered. "Find a seat, kids." He moved quickly down the aisle.

The train car had grown dim. The train began to slow, then came to a stop.

"We'll be on our way in a minute, everyone," the conductor announced. "Please stay where you are."

KC dropped into an empty seat, and Marshall took one across the aisle. None of the other passengers seemed to care that the train had stopped. One man held a small flashlight to see his book.

KC was thinking about what she'd write in her journal, when the lights blinked back on. The train began to move.

"Okay, let's go," KC said. She reached the door first and yanked it open. They stepped across the narrow connecting platform, and Marshall opened the next door.

The snack car was bright and cheerful. There was a row of tables on the right, under the windows. The tables were covered with crisp white tablecloths. In the middle of each table, a small silver tray held jars of mustard and ketchup. Blue and gold menus stood between salt and pepper shakers. Gleaming knives, forks, and spoons lay next to folded napkins.

At one of the tables, two men sat playing cards. Both wore baseball caps. One of the men stared at KC and Marshall as they passed.

KC felt funny with her hair tucked under her own cap. She wondered if anyone would recognize her as the president's stepdaughter.

She and Marshall kept walking.

"I smell pizza!" Marshall said. "Maybe I'll change my order."

Across from the tables was a long counter. Signs hung on the wall behind it, telling passengers what food and drinks they could buy. Under the signs, KC saw a row of tall storage cupboards. Candy bars and bags of peanuts and chips were displayed on the counter.

Suddenly a woman's head popped up from behind the counter.

"Sorry, I didn't see you," she said.

The woman was short and thick around the middle. She had blond hair and narrow glasses that sat on the end of her nose. Her bright red lipstick matched her uniform jacket. A name tag was pinned to the front. It said MANDY.

"What can I get you?" Mandy asked.

KC pulled out her list. "We'd like three coffees, one orange juice, and one grape soda," she said.

"Aren't you a little young for coffee?" Mandy asked KC.

"They're not for us," Marshall piped up. "They're for the vice—"

"My aunt and uncle," KC interrupted. "And my other aunt. Oh, and one tuna sandwich, please."

"What's in the coffees?" Mandy asked.

"Um, two are black, and one is with cream," KC said.

"The cream will be on the side," Mandy said. She turned to the coffeepot, which was behind her. It took a couple of minutes for her to fill three paper cups, snap on lids, and set the coffees into a carrying tray. "Anything else?"

"Yes, please, a slice of cheese pizza!" Marshall said.

Mandy slid a slice of pizza into a microwave. When the bell went off, she placed the slice on the tray with the tuna

FOOD
Orioles

sandwich and drinks. She rang up the order on a small cash register. "That'll be fourteen twenty-five," she said.

KC handed her the twenty.

Mandy pulled out the change, which she gave to KC.

KC wondered if she was supposed to tip, and how much. In her hand, she held three quarters and a five-dollar bill.

Then she noticed a metal dish on the counter with some coins in it. She dropped the quarters into the plate.

"Thanks, kids," Mandy said.

"You're welcome," KC said. She picked up the carrying tray.

"Is it heavy?" Marshall asked. "Wait a sec." He lifted out his soda and pizza.

"It's okay," KC said. "Let's just hope the lights don't go out again!"

3
KC Sees a Mystery

They walked past the men playing cards. KC stumbled a little as the train lurched beneath her, but she kept her balance.

"Don't drop it," one of the men said.

"I won't," KC answered. "Marsh, can you get the door?"

They walked carefully through the next car. At the end, the blind man was passing his fingers over a page in his book. KC wondered what he was doing, then realized he must be reading Braille.

Across from him, the woman still slept, wrapped in her blanket.

Marshall opened the door, and they both stepped onto the swaying platform that connected this car to their own.

KC giggled. “My feet want to go one way, but my body has other ideas!” she said.

Marshall opened the final door, and they were back in the vice president’s car.

“Hurray, coffee!” Mary Kincaid said. “Any problems?”

“Only the lights going off,” Marshall said.

Robert took the cardboard tray from KC’s hands. Janet passed out the coffees and the vice president’s sandwich. KC took her juice and sat facing forward, across from Marshall.

KC pulled off her cap. Then she remembered the five-dollar bill. She stood up and walked back to Mary Kincaid. “Here’s the change,” she said. “Stuff on the train is expensive! I tipped the lady seventy-five cents. Was that okay?”

"Perfect," the vice president said. "Thanks for doing that, KC."

KC walked back to her seat. "Where's your pizza?" she asked Marshall.

He grinned. "Gone to tummy land."

"Already?" KC asked.

Marshall let out a small burp.

KC sat back and sipped her orange juice. She took a book out of her backpack. It was a nonfiction book about Pennsylvania. "We're going to Lancaster," she said. "That's where Ms. Kincaid's farm is."

She leaned forward to show Marshall some pictures. "There are these people there called Amish," she said. "They don't have electricity or drive cars."

"How do they watch TV and use computers?" Marshall asked.

"They don't," KC said. "And instead of

cars, they have horses and buggies. When it gets dark, they use candles or kerosene lamps. Look, here's a picture of one of the buggies. Read what it says about no electricity."

"I can't look," Marshall said. "I'll puke if I try to read."

"That's because you're riding backward," KC said. "Sit next to me so you're facing the same way the train is traveling. You won't get sick. Here, you can be next to the window."

Marshall sat next to KC. Now they were both facing the door.

"I wonder if blind people get sick when they read Braille on a train," KC said.

"What made you think of that?" Marshall asked. "That guy in the next car?"

KC nodded. "Yes," she said. "He's facing

this car, the same direction you were sitting. Most people sit facing forward, the same direction the train is moving. But he's sitting backward."

"But if he's blind—" Marshall started to say.

"And you know what else?" KC said. "The woman across the aisle from him is sitting the same way. They're both facing this car."

"So maybe they know the vice president is in this car, and they're just curious," Marshall suggested.

KC shook her head. "Nobody knows she's here," she said.

"I think the conductors know," said Marshall.

"Well, maybe, but no one else," KC said.

The kids rode in silence for a few

minutes. Outside the windows, scenery flashed by. KC held her book, but she wasn't reading.

"You're still thinking about it, aren't you?" Marshall asked.

"Thinking about what?" KC asked.

He laughed. "You know what. It's bugging you that two people are facing the wrong way on a train," he said. "You're trying to make some mystery out of it, the way you always do."

"I do not make mysteries," KC said.

"Do too."

"You always accuse me of that," KC said.

"That's because it's true," Marshall said. "Even your mom says you have a very active imagination. I've heard her!"

KC tried not to smile. She lifted her book and began reading.

"How long before we get there?" Marshall asked.

"Over an hour," KC said. "Why didn't you bring a book to read?"

"I told you, I get sick when I read on trains," Marshall said.

KC looked at him. "Marsh, you said this was your first train ride!"

"It is, but still." He shrugged.

KC kept reading.

Marshall sighed. He bent down and tied one of his sneaker laces. Then he breathed on the window glass to make it fog over and wrote his name. He wiped his name away, breathed on the glass again, and drew a picture of a spider. "I should have brought Spike," he said.

"Spike? I don't think you can bring tarantulas on a train," KC said.

"Why not? That guy in the next car brought his dog," Marshall said.

KC laughed. "That's different," she said. "It's a Seeing Eye dog. The man needs him."

"Well, I need Spike," Marshall said. "He keeps me company."

"Don't I keep you company?" KC asked. "Do you like your old spider better than me?"

"Spike is a tarantula, not a regular spider," Marshall said. "And no, I don't like him better. I just like his . . . furry legs."

KC let out a laugh. She turned around. The vice president and the two agents had their eyes closed.

"We could go for a walk," KC said quietly.

"Where?" Marshall asked.

"Let's count how many cars there are," KC suggested.

Marshall hopped up. “Okay, anything is better than watching you read.”

“You should’ve brought a book,” KC said.

Marshall let out a big, fake sigh. He opened the door that led to the next car. Stepping forward, he nearly bumped into a man in gray work clothes. The man was crouched on the floor with a wrench in his hand. Next to him was an open toolbox.

The man looked up at the kids. “Always something to fix,” he said, shaking his head. He had lifted out part of the platform floor. Looking down, KC and Marshall could see the ground rushing beneath their feet. Dusty wind blew up around them.

Stepping past the man, KC opened the door, and they moved into the next car. Marshall nudged KC and made a goofy face. The sleeping woman still slept, facing

the kids. Across from her, the blind man was also asleep. KC could see her reflection in the man's dark glasses. His dog was snoozing on the floor.

The other people were still napping or reading or working on laptops. Near the end of the car, another man in gray work clothes was fixing something inside an electric panel on the wall over an empty seat. The door to the panel was open when KC and Marshall walked past. KC saw about a thousand tiny wires of all different colors.

The kids went into the snack car. It was empty. The tablecloths had been removed, and the tables were bare. KC saw a small sign on the counter. She read it out loud: "THE ATTENDANT WILL RETURN SHORTLY."

"Wow, she just left all this food sitting

out here," Marshall said. The candy, chips, and peanuts were on the counter. There was also a tray of ketchup and mustard bottles from the tables.

"Don't even think about it," KC said.

"I wasn't thinking about taking anything!" Marshall said. "Talk about people accusing other people of things!"

"Let's keep going," KC said. They walked through the next couple of cars. Passengers slept or read or chatted with each other. Some had earbuds in their ears, listening to music. One woman was knitting something blue. It wasn't quite dark outside, so some people stared out at the scenery.

"How many cars have we been in?" Marshall asked.

"This next one is six, I think, if we count our car," KC said.

At the end of the last car, they came to a door that wouldn't open. A small brass sign read, NO ADMITTANCE. ENGINEER ONLY.

"I guess this door must lead to the engine," KC said. She tried peeking through the small window, but it had been blackened.

"I wonder what it's like to drive a train," Marshall said.

"I don't think I'd want to try it," KC said. "Too fast!"

"Bet you'd like a horse and buggy," Marshall teased. "Like in your book—"

Suddenly the lights went out. KC felt the train begin to slow down. Then there was a shudder, and the floor jerked under their feet. The train stopped moving.

"Not again," Marshall said.

"At least there's still a little light coming through the windows," KC said. "We'd better sit down."

They took two empty seats.

"The windows are gross," Marshall said. He tried to wipe the window next to his seat, but the grime was on the outside. "Hey, look out there!"

KC leaned over Marshall and peered through the dim glass. She saw people on the ground, running toward the back of the train. Two seconds later, the runners were out of view.

Something tugged at KC's memory. Even seen through the dirty glass, one of the runners looked familiar.

Just then KC heard the door behind her open. Two conductors raced past the kids, heading down the aisle. One was bald, and the other had a mustache and curly hair. One side of his mustache hung crookedly over his lip.

"What's going on?" Marshall asked KC.

KC kept her eyes on the conductors as they disappeared into the next car. "I don't know," she said.

Other passengers began to talk to each other. A few had gotten out of their seats.

"Come on," KC said. "Aunt Kitty will wonder where we are."

KC and Marshall hurried down the aisle. They had to excuse themselves several times because people were standing in the aisle, trying to figure out what was happening.

They passed through the snack car, but Mandy was still missing. Her sign was on the counter. A couple of passengers were standing there, wondering how to get served.

The lights came on suddenly, and soon the train began moving. A few people clapped and whistled.

The kids walked through the final car before their own. The two conductors were there, blocking the aisle. The bald one held up his hand as KC and Marshall approached.

"Whoa, where are you going?" he asked.

"To our car," KC said. "It's the next one."

The conductor shook his head. "You must be mistaken," he said.

The second conductor, the one with the mustache, nodded. "This is the last car," he said.

KC couldn't believe what she was hearing. "But we were in that car," she said. "The . . . my aunt is in there. She's waiting for us!"

"Sorry, kid," the bald conductor said.

"There is no other car. Look for yourself."

He stepped aside so KC could see through the little window in the door behind him. KC peered through the glass. Without thinking, she pushed back her baseball cap so she could see better. She gasped at what she saw—railroad tracks falling away behind the train, with trees and bushes on both sides of the tracks.

But there was no cute caboose car. There were no blue leather seats. No little tables. No vice president or secret service agents.

Marshall looked, too. His mouth fell open.

KC felt like she was having a nightmare and she'd wake up any second. But it wasn't a nightmare. A whole train car had vanished. And with it, so had the vice president of the United States!

4
Where to Hide

KC turned quickly and looked at the two seats nearest herself and Marshall and the conductors. The blind man, his dog, and the sleeping woman were gone.

KC stood staring at the empty seats, thinking. Then she turned back to the conductors. She smiled. "I feel like a dope," she said. "You're right. We're in the wrong car. Come on, Marsh."

KC grabbed Marshall's arm and pulled him up the aisle.

"KC, what're you doing?" he protested. "Those guys—"

"Shhh!" KC said. She yanked Marshall into the next car. KC ran up the aisle, past the snack counter, still clasping Marshall's arm.

"Will someone tell me what's going on?" Marshall said.

"We have to hide!" KC whispered.

At the end of the car, KC shoved open the small door that led to the platform. Warm air blew into their faces.

"KC, what are we doing?" Marshall asked. "What's going on?"

"I think they kidnapped the vice president, Marsh!" KC hissed.

"What? Are you kidding? Who kidnapped her?" Marshall asked.

"Not now!" KC whispered back.

She pulled Marshall through the next door. Slowing down, they walked along the aisle. KC looked at each person they passed. When they came to a bathroom, she yanked Marshall inside. It was barely big enough for them to stand facing each other. KC flipped the door lock to the "shut" position.

"I don't know how they did it," KC said. "But they took the car off the train. Our car is gone!"

KC's heart was racing. Her hands felt cold, and she couldn't get them to stop shaking. In the mirror, she saw her face. It was white, and her freckles looked bigger than normal. Some of her hair had escaped from under her cap. She tucked it back and yanked the cap on tighter.

"But who?" Marshall asked.

"I think it was that blind guy and the woman sitting near him," KC said. "Only he isn't really blind. And she wasn't really sleeping! They were watching us the whole time! And they're gone, too!"

"How could they make the train car disappear?" Marshall asked. "This is crazy, KC!"

"I know it's crazy!" KC said. "But it happened. The car is gone! They must have . . . wait a minute! There was a guy messing around on the platform, remember? He could have unhooked the car when the train stopped the last time!"

"Yeah, the lights were out for about five minutes," Marshall said.

KC nodded. "That's when they did it!" she said. "And remember when we looked out the window and saw people running next to the train while it was stopped? I thought one of them looked familiar. I think he was the guy on the platform outside the vice president's car. And the other one could be the man who was fixing something in one of those electric boxes on the wall. They made the lights go out so the engineer would stop the train!"

"So they . . . so we . . . I'm so mixed up!" Marshall said. He tried again. "Where are they, I mean the guys who did it? And where's the vice president and the secret service agents?"

"I don't know," KC said. "The car must be behind us somewhere."

"So then why are we hiding?" Marshall asked. "We have to tell someone!"

"No!" KC said. "There might be other people in on it! Anyone on this train could be after us!"

"What do you mean, after us?" Marshall asked. "They don't even know who we are!"

"Me, Marsh," KC said. "They might want to kidnap the president's stepdaughter!

They figured out that Aunt Kitty was really the vice president, so maybe they also know who I am. Especially because I was dumb enough to shove my hat back and show my hair in front of those two conductors!"

"If the conductors kidnapped the vice president," Marshall asked, "why didn't they grab *us* a few minutes ago?"

"I don't know, but we can't take any chances. Those conductors seemed nice, but they could both be imposters!" KC said. "Somehow they learned that the vice president takes this train a lot. They planned the whole thing, maybe with help from those guys in the gray work clothes. They stopped the train and unhooked the car with the vice president in it!"

"Gee, I don't know," Marshall said. "Maybe you're just—"

“Don’t you dare tell me it’s my imagination, Marshall!” KC said. “A train car disappeared. Is that my imagination?”

Suddenly the door handle rattled. Someone was trying to get into the restroom. Then KC and Marshall heard a knock on the door.

“Anyone in there?” a man’s deep voice asked.

5
A Tight Squeeze

KC jumped when she heard the voice. She shook her head so Marshall wouldn't say anything.

The knock came again, then the voice. "Hello? Anyone inside?"

KC thought furiously. Should they answer or not? That could be one of the kidnappers outside the door!

"Yeah, I'm in here," Marshall answered in a gruff voice. "Gimme a few minutes, man! I'm feeling sick!" Then he made a noise like he was throwing up.

Outside the door, the voice said, "Okay, cool. Good luck, dude!"

KC waited a minute. Then she gave him

a high five. “Nice going, Marsh,” she said.

Marshall grinned. “Anytime.”

“But we can’t stay here,” KC went on. “If I’m right about those two conductors, they’ll be looking for us.”

“You mean the fake conductors, right?”

KC nodded.

“You could call the president,” Marshall suggested. “He’ll get the FBI to stop the train and rescue us!”

“I can’t call him,” KC said. “My cell phone is in my backpack. It was on my seat in the vice president’s train car.”

“Oh,” Marshall said. “So maybe we can borrow someone else’s phone. Just go tell one of the other passengers who you are, and they’ll let you—”

“Marsh, we can’t talk to anyone!” KC said. “We don’t know who the bad guys are. I think that blind man and the sleeping woman were in disguises, pretending to be just passengers. They're part of the plot."

"So what do we do?" Marshall asked. "Sooner or later, someone will want to use this bathroom."

"I know," KC groaned. "I'm thinking."

Marshall closed his eyes. "I can't believe this is happening," he said.

"Okay, here's what we do," KC said. "We have to hide somewhere really good. We stay there till we get to Lancaster, then we get off with everyone else. We'll find a phone, and I'll call the White House."

"Okay, but where do we hide?" Marshall asked. "There aren't a lot of choices, you know."

"I have one idea," KC said.

"Will I like it?" Marshall asked.

"You'll love it," KC said. "We'll hide in the snack car."

"Where?" Marshall asked.

"I saw some tall cubboards behind the counter," KC said. "They should be big enough for us to squeeze into. We'll stay there until we get to Lancaster."

"But what about the woman who works there, what's her name?" Marshall asked. "What'll we tell her?"

"Mandy. I don't know where she is, but I think the snack car is shut down," KC said. "Remember that sign?"

"Yeah, it said she'd be back shortly!" Marshall said.

"So we'd better hurry up," KC said. She unlocked the bathroom door and cracked it open a half inch. She saw a few passengers in their seats, but no one was looking in her direction.

KC stepped out of the bathroom and Marshall followed her.

They tried to look as if they weren't worried about anything. But KC's stomach was trembling and her hands felt cold.

They passed an old man sitting near the aisle. He was reading a newspaper and not paying attention to the kids walking past. White hair poked out from under his hat. His coat covered his lap and feet.

Next to him was a college student. He was listening to music. His head bopped to whatever tune he was hearing.

KC and Marshall reached the snack car. It looked the same. The tables had no cloths or napkins. The sign was on the counter.

"Perfect," KC said as she zipped behind

the counter and ducked down. "Marsh, come on!"

Marshall joined her behind the counter. KC was on her knees, opening cupboards. Most were filled with stuff like napkins, ketchup, paper cups and plates, and plastic knives, forks, and spoons.

"Here, this one," KC said. "Just a few folded tablecloths."

"Can we both fit?" Marshall asked.

"We have to!" KC said. "Wait till I shove this stuff aside." She climbed into the cupboard. When she sat with her knees folded, there was plenty of room. "Come on in!"

Marshall crawled into the cupboard, facing KC. The toes of their sneakers were touching. KC reached out and pulled the door shut.

"Now we just wait," she whispered.

"When we get to Lancaster, we'll mix in with some other people and get off."

"How will we know when we're there?" Marshall asked.

"We're there when the train stops," KC said. She wiggled around to get more comfortable.

"But what if the lights go off again, and the train has to stop before we get to Lancaster?" Marshall asked.

"Oh, I didn't think of that," KC said.

They both sat silently in the cupboard. It was dark inside, and there wasn't much air.

"We should have picked the cupboard where they keep the candy," Marshall said.

"The conductors will announce it when we get to Lancaster," KC said.

"They will?" Marshall asked.

"When I took the train to Florida, the

conductors let us know every time we came to a different station," KC said. "They just walked through the cars telling people to get ready to get off."

"But those were friendly conductors," Marshall said. "If you're right about these two conductors, they're kidnappers!"

"Oh, I didn't think of that, either," KC said.

Marshall let out a little moan.

6
Ketchup or Mustard?

"KC, what if you're wrong?" Marshall asked. "What if the vice president wasn't really kidnapped? Couldn't the car have gotten unhitched by accident?"

KC wished she could stretch her legs. She was getting cramped sitting in this small, dark cupboard. "Then how do you explain the other weird things that happened?" she asked.

"Like what?"

"Like that blind man and his dog disappearing, and that woman who was sleeping across from him," KC said. "Where are they? And what about that guy who was messing around between the two cars, just a few minutes before our car got unhooked? And who were those people we saw running outside the train?"

"Well, maybe the vice president and Robert and Janet escaped," Marshall said. "They'll call the Air Force or something!"

"This isn't a movie," KC said. "This is . . . listen, what's that?"

KC pressed her ear against the cupboard door. Then she leaned forward to whisper to Marshall. "I think someone is out there. I heard a voice!"

". . . president's kid is gone," one voice said. "The boss isn't gonna like this."

"But why would the girl run?" the other one asked. "She doesn't know we're after her."

"They figured it out," the first voice said. "We'll find them. Let's check every seat and every bathroom. Look in the luggage racks above the seats. We'll meet back here, okay?"

"Got it," the other voice said.

KC waited a few minutes before speaking. Her heart was thumping so loud she was sure Marshall could hear it. "Did you hear them?" she whispered finally.

"Yeah," Marshall whispered back. "They know who you are, and they know we know they know!"

"We can't stay in here," KC said. "When they don't find us anywhere else on the train, they're bound to check these cupboards."

"If only we could get inside the engine car," Marshall said. "We could lock ourselves in and tell the engineer what's going on."

"Marsh, the engineer could be in on it, too," KC said. "He could be the 'boss' that guy was talking about! The engineer was the one who stopped the train when the lights went out."

"Do you know what Spider-Man would do?" Marshall asked.

KC grinned in the dark. She knew Marshall was trying to joke around because he was scared.

"He'd throw out some web and jump up on the ceiling," Marshall went on. "Then, when the bad guys walked under him, he'd drop down and—"

"Marsh, that's a great idea!" KC said. "We could hide inside the ceiling! It might be hollow!"

"How do you know?" Marshall asked.

"The top of the train is rounded, but the car ceilings are flat," KC said. "So there must be space up there."

"We can't reach it," Marshall said.

"We'll stand on the counter," KC said. She opened the cupboard door enough to see that they were alone in the snack car. "Come on, Marsh."

The kids crawled out of their hiding space. KC stretched. It felt good to unfold her legs.

"Stand by the door so you can see through the window if they're coming," KC said.

"Which door?" Marshall asked. "There are two!"

"Both!" KC said.

She climbed up on the counter. Now that she was closer, the square ceiling panels looked like they could be moved. But she wasn't tall enough. Even with her arms and hands outstretched and standing

FOOD

on tiptoes, KC couldn't touch the panels.

"KC, one of the conductors is coming!" Marshall hissed. He ran behind the counter and pulled open the cupboard door.

"No, they're bound to search those!" KC said.

Then she noticed the laundry cart. The cart was tall and wide and had four wheels. It was half-filled with tablecloths and napkins that had been removed from the tables. KC doubted there were washing machines on the train. That meant the laundry cart would be wheeled off the train so the dirty stuff could be washed.

"Jump into that cart!" she whispered to Marshall. "Get under the tablecloths!"

Marshall hesitated only a second, then he leaped into the cart. He buried himself in the soiled linens.

KC started to join him, then stopped. What if they checked under the tablecloths? She looked around the snack car. Was there another, better hiding place?

The bottles of ketchup and mustard on the counter gave her an idea. She pulled a clean tablecoth from the cupboard where they'd been hiding. Unfolding the cloth, she shook globs of ketchup all over its white surface. Then she jumped into the cart and pulled the ketchup-stained cloth over her head.

Praying the kidnappers wouldn't want to get ketchup on their hands, she tried to burrow down next to Marshall.

A moment later, she heard the whoosh of air that let her know the snack car door had been opened.

7
Trapped

KC and Marshall were jammed next to each other in the bottom of the linen cart. KC could feel Marshall's elbow in her side. One of his feet poked her chin.

KC could also hear the phony conductor's footsteps. He was only a few feet away from the cart. She thought he was alone, because he wasn't talking.

Then she heard something else. It was a cupboard door being opened. Then it slammed shut. She heard another door open and shut. He was searching the cupboards where they had been hiding!

"There you are," a man said. "Find anything?"

"No," another voice answered. "But these cupboards are big enough to hide in. Hey, what's this?"

"Baseball cap," the first voice said. "Orioles."

KC gasped. Her cap! It must have fallen off while they were in the linen cupboard.

"Yeah, it was here in this cupboard. The last time I saw it, she was wearing it," his pal said. "The president's stepkid."

"They were here?" the first voice said. "So where'd they go?"

"I don't know," answered the other voice. "But they can't get away. They're trapped on this train."

Several other cupboards were opened, then closed. KC couldn't tell if they were coming closer to the cart or moving farther away.

"Shove that cart out of the way," one of the men said. "There's another cupboard behind it."

KC froze. She held her breath. She felt the cart being jerked out of the way. Then it stopped moving.

"Hey, come 'ere," one of the voices said. "I think we may have just hit the jackpot."

Suddenly the tablecloths on top of KC and Marshall were yanked away. The kids were no longer hidden. They looked up and saw two faces staring down at them. It was the two "conductors" who'd lied to them about the vice president's car.

"Well, lookee here," the bald one said. He dropped KC's cap into the cart. "Did you lose this?"

KC opened her mouth, but nothing

came out. Marshall's face appeared from under the tablecloths.

"Don't even think of screaming," the man with the mustache said. He glanced at his watch. "We'll be getting to the station in a few minutes. Till then, this is probably the best place for you."

"You won't get away with this!" Marshall finally said. "Do you know who her step-father is?"

"We sure do, kid," the bald man said. "Why else do you think we're doing all this?"

"If you let us go, the president will be grateful," KC said. She was trying to sound calm, but inside she was terrified. "He won't put you in jail!"

"Nice try, kid," the bald man said. He yanked KC out of the cart and tied a cloth napkin around her mouth. Then he used another one to bind her hands behind her back.

KC watched as the other man did the same to Marshall. Then the men dropped the kids back into the cart.

"Nighty-night," the man with the mustache said. Tablecloths were dumped on top of them. "Pretty soon we'll take you for a nice car ride."

"Okay," the other voice said. "We have to go play conductor again. We need to let the passengers know we're coming into Lancaster station. These two will be safe till we get back."

KC heard footsteps walking away. She could only see white tablecloths around her face. She smelled ketchup. One of Marshall's feet was jammed against her cheek. She felt the rough tread of his sneaker.

Then there was silence, except for her own heart beating and Marshall's breathing.

KC lay covered with dirty tablecloths. A napkin was tied around her head, right across her mouth. Marshall's foot was wiggling, tapping against her head. Was he trying to send her a signal?

KC bumped her head against his foot. His sneaker nudged her again. They were having a conversation!

Then KC had an idea. She scraped her napkin gag against the bottom of Marshall's sneaker. The napkin moved slightly. She tried again, and the gag slipped even more. After a few more tries, she was able to force the napkin down over her chin. Her mouth felt dry. What she wouldn't give for Marshall's grape soda!

"Marshall?" she whispered. "Are you okay?"

The foot tapped the side of her head.

KC smiled. "Don't worry, we—"

Suddenly KC heard something strange. It sounded like a little kid whimpering. The sound was coming from just outside the laundry cart.

Then something was scratching the cart. It moved on its wheels.

"KC?" a soft voice said. "Can you hear me? This is Secret Service Agent Daniels. We're here to help you. We know you and your friend are in this cart."

The layer of tablecloths was removed. KC looked up into a man's face. He seemed concerned, but he was smiling. Next to him was a large German shepherd.

Its dark eyes looked at KC. Its long tongue hung out of its mouth.

"They unhooked the vice president's car—" KC started to say.

"We know," Agent Daniels said. "The vice president is safe. You'll be with her soon."

Then there was another face looking down at KC. It was a woman with red hair. "Hi, I'm Agent Miranda."

KC grinned.

While Agent Daniels kept watch, Agent Miranda untied both kids' hands and removed Marshall's gag.

"They're coming back!" Agent Daniels said. "I see them in the next car, headed this way!"

"We have to hide!" Agent Miranda said.

"Try the linen cupboard," KC said.

"Got it," Agent Daniels said. He flipped

a tablecloth over KC and Marshall, then disappeared behind the snack counter.

The door whooshed open.

"Okay, let's get this cart ready," one of the phony conductors said.

KC heard doors crashing open. Agent Daniels yelled, "Freeze!"

"Don't even think of moving!" Agent Miranda added. "Flat on the floor—now! Hands behind your backs—now!"

KC heard thumps and grunts. A dog growled and barked.

Then Agent Miranda's friendly voice said, "Okay, kids, it's all over."

Suddenly Marshall's head popped up out of the tablecloths. "What did I miss?" he asked.

8
Guardian Angels

KC, Marshall, and Mary Kincaid were eating a picnic lunch on the vice president's back porch in Lancaster, Pennsylvania. Her dog, Bounder, lay at their feet. In a nearby pasture, three horses nibbled grass behind a white fence. Twenty feet away, Secret Service Agents Janet and Robert sat in the shade, eating hamburgers and drinking lemonade.

"There were six kidnappers," the vice president said. "Mandy was the boss. She persuaded her two brothers to mess with the electricity and unhitch our car from the train. They wore gray work clothes so they'd look like part of the regular train crew."

"We saw them!" KC said. "And two of the others were those guys pretending to be conductors?"

"That's right," the vice president said. "The one with the shaved head was a real conductor, but he was in on the plot. The other one wore a fake mustache to look like the other real conductor. Those two are actually cousins, Bud and Karl Fester. And the engineer was in on it, too."

"What happened to the conductor with the real mustache?" Marshall asked. He wiped some ketchup from his mouth.

"He was tied up and left in the train car with Janet, Robert, and me," the vice president explained. "We figure that Mandy put something in our coffees to make us sleep, before the car was unhooked. Mandy and her two brothers climbed into the car with us, but we didn't know that until we woke up."

"So Bud and Karl stayed on the train to kidnap Marshall and me," KC said. "I guess they decided not to grab us where people were watching."

"Yes, they were supposed to bring you to some house they had rented to hide all of us," Mary Kincaid said. "Then they'd contact the White House and demand money. But Janet and Robert were able to overpower Mandy and her brothers. Your two abductors didn't know that, of course. They thought we were on our way to their safe house."

"But who are Agents Miranda and Daniels?" Marshall asked.

"I think I know!" KC said. "Agent Miranda was disguised as the sleeping woman in the train car near ours, right? And Agent Daniels was the blind man with the Seeing Eye dog."

The vice president nodded. "Anyone want the last burger?" she asked.

"No thank you, Ms. Kincaid," KC said.

"I'm full," Marshall said, rubbing his stomach. "But I'll want it in five minutes!"

"KC, you're right about Agents Daniels and Miranda," the vice president said. "The president put them on the train to keep an eye on you two kids while Janet and Robert stayed with me."

"Where are Agents Miranda and Daniels now?" Marshall asked.

Mary Kincaid gazed out toward the barn that stood next to the pasture. "Not far away," she said. "I'll let you in on a little secret. Agents Miranda and Daniels are

never far from you two, no matter where you go."

"They follow us?" Marshall asked. "Cool!"

"How come we've never noticed them before?" KC asked.

The vice president laughed. "They're both masters at disguising themselves," she said. "They changed their disguises on the train because they needed to stay near you. Remember the old man with white hair who had a big old overcoat?"

"Wait a minute, was he sitting next to a college kid with earphones?" KC asked.

The vice president nodded. "Agent Miranda was the old man," she said. "Their rescue dog, Pete, was at her feet, hidden under the coat."

"And I'll bet the college kid was really

Agent Daniels, right?" Marshall asked.

"That's right," Mary Kincaid said. "The president has ordered them to stay with you whenever you leave the White House. Those two are your guardian angels."

Just then KC heard a thudding noise over the house. It was a familiar sound. She ran off the porch and looked up. A helicopter was preparing to land next to the barn.

"Hey, Marsh!" KC yelled. "It's the president! Don't eat that last hamburger!"

Did you know?

Did you know that Andrew Jackson was the first president to travel by train? He rode twelve miles from Ellicott's Mills, Maryland, to Baltimore in 1833.

President Abraham Lincoln took some very important train rides. One, in 1863, was fro Washington, D.C., to Gettysburg, Pennsylvania There, he gave one of the most famous speeches of all time, the Gettysburg Address But President Lincoln's final train ride was very sad. He was assassinated in 1865. A train carried his coffin from Washington to his home in Springfield, Illinois. Along the way, it stopped at thirteen cities, where citizens paid their respects. Presidents Franklin Roosevelt and Dwight Eisenhower also had funeral trains many years later.

Warren G. Harding was the first president to visit Alaska, which was a territory when he took a train there in 1923. Alaska's railroad was brand-new at the time. In Fairbanks, visitors can see the train car the president rode.

People still love to ride the train—even presidents! President Barack Obama took a train to his inauguration in 2009. A special car built in 1939 was hooked to the back end. People gathered near the tracks to wave to him as his train passed by.